A
Little
Tail

Liz Wise

DEDICATION

To all the real students at E.R. Andrews Elementary School. Thank you for helping me write this book. You inspire me every day.

My beautiful nieces and nephews; Evan, Marissa, Noah, Bella, Ben, Rachel, Ezra, Eli, Ethan, Hope, Isaiah, Emilia, and Aaron. I love you to the moon and back.

To the real Paisley and my precious Cowboy. Thank you for always showing me unconditional love.

"The world would be a nicer place if everyone had the ability to love as unconditionally as a dog." — M.K. Clinton

ACKNOWLEDGMENTS

To the grown-ups I made read this book first. Thank you. You are such amazing human beings and I'm so lucky to have you in my life.

To my wonderful mama, thank you for always believing in me and constantly encouraging me to chase my dreams.

Hope

It's getting dark outside. I can see the shadow of the old pine tree outside my bedroom window reflecting on the wall. I hear the cricket's sweet song echoing in the distance and imagine that the breathtaking view of the fireflies dancing out in the backyard.

It seems like it could be a beautiful sight.

A beautiful dream.

If only I could see it.

Inside, it's so far from that. Mom is yelling. Dad is screaming. I run into my closet and slam the door. I don't know why I slam it, they can't hear me anyway.

I hold my hands over my ears, hoping to drown out the sound. The tears start to pour from my eyes and I can't get them to stop. My stomach pains with hunger, but I ignore it. That's nothing to compare to the pain in my heart.

I'm seven years old. This is not the same life I know my friends have. They don't cry all by themselves in a closet.

They don't go to bed hungry.
Or scared.
Or sad.
Or do they?

Jillie

I'm really not sure why Mom decided it was a good idea to pack up all our things in a big moving truck and move all the way across the country. I was perfectly content living in an apartment in the city. Texas was warm and busy. There was always something to do. We had a pool right inside our apartment building. I could go swimming all the time, even when it was raining.

But Mom had to go, "follow her dreams," and Dad said, "we have to be supportive." So now here we are in the middle of nowhere, surrounded by farms, and trees, and wide-open spaces. It smells like dirt and cow poop. I just want to go back to my friends in Texas and my indoor pool.

Oh. Did I forget to mention that the closest pool to my house is thirty-five minutes away? That is a very long time to wait to go swimming.

So far, we've been here three weeks and I haven't even seen another child. Do they even have a school around here?

Stuart

"STUART RYAN MURPHY!!!!"

I hear my mother's scream from outside. I'm not exactly sure why she is yelling. Is it because I used plastic wrap to cover the toilet seat or is it the spicy peppercorn I put in her coveted mint chocolate chip ice cream? I picture her face when she realized the cool and refreshing mint ice cream was being overtaken by the spicy red peppercorn and how she probably drank a whole bottle of water to defeat the heat.

Sometimes, I really love my life.

"STUART!" I hear her yell again, so I make my way into the house. She's not standing in the kitchen and there isn't a bowl of ice cream in sight. I walk past the bathroom and the plastic wrap is still covering the porcelain throne. I decide to holler back, but before I can my mouth is frozen as I walk to where my mom is standing.

Right by the front door.

And there is a person on the porch.
And that person looks mad.
And that person is making me nervous.
And that person is making my heart pace and my palms sweat.
And that person is about to change my whole life.

Forever.

That person is a cop.

Paz

My mom named me Paz because she read somewhere that it means, "peace." I came into the world at a time where her life was anything but peaceful. She once wrote down that I was the calming force that could get her through all the storms of her life. I wish that was the truth. I couldn't get her through all the challenges that she faced.

She died before my third birthday.

I know her face, because my Uncle G shows me pictures. I know how funny she was because of the stories he tells. I know she got him through all the hardships that he faced.

I know that because he tells me. He tells me that the least he could do to pay her back was to take care of me for everything she did for him. He tells me that she saved his life, but we don't talk about how she died. I've never even seen where she's laid to rest. He tells me that's not what I need to remember.

But what I remember is all my friend's at school talk about their moms. Their dads. Their brothers. Their sisters. And the only thing I have is a crazy uncle and a faded photograph of my mother.

That's my family.

Harper

I'm not exactly sure what I am supposed to write. I wasn't given any guidelines. There wasn't a rubric to follow or a detailed outline specifically laying out everything I needed to discuss. So, I'm taking this time to write a story about a glittery unicorn named Rainbow Sparkles.

Once upon a time there was a unicorn named Rainbow Sparkles. She was a kind-hearted unicorn that would do anything for anyone.

Do you need a ride across town to go the grocery store to buy sour jelly beans? Rainbow Sparkles can help.

Do you need a dozen cupcakes for a birthday party? (Rainbow can help, but please don't ask where she got them from. Trust me you don't want to know.)

One day, Rainbow Sparkles was galloping through the flowery meadow when mean Drake the Dragon tried to steal her Rainbow shiny mane. Rainbow Sparkles did the only thing she knew how to defeat the terrible dragon. She....

Paisley

It's really cold tonight and I'm really hungry. I could go to my usual spot. The empty parking lot behind the restaurant that serves those long potato pieces that the children call, "french fries." I don't know why they are called "french fries." The only French I know is the French Bulldog that used to live next door to me at my old house. His name was Chester. His parents used to ask if Chester went, "Oui Oui," outside. Whatever that means. Seriously though, do you know what that means?

I usually fill up on old garbage from the restaurant. Sometimes the workers shoo me off, but there is one man who always sneaks a burger or two my way. One time, when I was extremely hungry, he pretended to trip outside while delivering a bagful of deliciousness to a little old lady's car. The bag of food went flying all the way over to the dumpster. I ate it up quickly.

I do a lot of things that I'm not supposed to do. I don't look both ways before crossing the street. (Thank goodness it's not a busy town). I chase squirrels up trees and bark at the mailman. I even broke into someone's house using their dog's doggy door. I didn't do it to be naughty, I just wanted to escape the cold and have someone rub my belly and tell me everything was going to be okay.

Even if I didn't think it ever could be again.

Miss Little

Dear Journal,

Today was a marvelous day for me. I just found out this morning that I got my first teaching job. My oh my, it is just so exciting. I have been waiting for this day for what seems like an eternity. I cannot believe it! The principal, Mrs. McGee, informed me that I was the new third grade teacher at Edward Ralph Anderson Elementary School.

All my dreams were coming true.

Mrs. McGee also told me that school starts in just two weeks. Two weeks. Wow. I better get going. I have lots of lessons to plan and a classroom to decorate.

I have fifteen children counting on me to teach them everything they need to know as third graders.

Eek.

Fondly,
Miss Little

Jillie

I know I shouldn't complain about school starting in two weeks. I've had an extra long summer vacation this year, almost a full three months. I guess that could be considered one positive thing about moving up north.

Probably the **only** positive thing.

It's been one long month since we've first arrived in our new hometown and I've only been to the pool once. That's right. Just. One. Time. I can't complain though at least dad took Carson and me to the pool.

I've told you about Carson, right?

Oh. I haven't.

Well, let me just tell you about my little brother Carson.

I found out about Carson three years ago. Except when I found about him, he was supposed to be Carrie. My beautiful little sister.

Mom painted a pink room with purple flowers around the walls. We went clothes shopping so Carrie and I could have matching outfits.

Mom even let me pick out the dress Carrie would wear home from the hospital.

Imagine my surprise when I went to meet my baby sister and found out it was a boy.

Ick. I was devastated.

And I've been upset about it ever since.

There were a few days in the beginning that I was starting to get use to the idea of liking my baby brother, but then he started keeping me up at night with his constant crying.

Seriously, I need my sleep or I get cranky.

If you thought the crying was bad, you should've been through his crawling years.

Goodbye favorite sunglasses. (He snapped you in half.)

Goodbye favorite teddy bear. (He decided to use you as a bathroom.)

Goodbye favorite squishy ball (He bit you so hard that you started oozing.)

But that wasn't even the worst thing that the Carson-monster did.

Not even close.

The worst thing he ever did was on the day of the big move. We had all gotten in our mini van. Dad was driving, Mom was giving directions, and Carson and I were watching one of Carson's baby shows in the back.

The show was not even half way through, when Carson decided to show us everything he ate for breakfast. I'm not joking when I tell you that there was throw up all over his seat, and my seat, and dad's seat, the floor, and even all over the ceiling.

How he managed to do that, I will never know.

"Pull the car over, Jack." I heard Mom yell.

"I can't Annie," he answered, "We are in the middle of a traffic jam."

I buried my head in my shirt as the disgusting smell of regurgitated eggs filled the air.

It felt like hours before we made it to a gas station so we could clean out the pukemobile. Mom took Carson to the bathroom and Dad started cleaning up the car.

"Here Jillian" he said to me as he handed me a roll of hand wipes. "Start cleaning up the floor, please."

"You're kidding, right?" I question, but he simply responds:

"Sometimes in a family we have to do things that are not easy, but messy and gross. This is just one of those gross times."

So, there I am, being all Cinderella like, when I feel a gurgle start rumbling in my stomach.

"Dad." I say, "I don't feel so well." and just as Dad looks up to see what I need, I pepper him with what I had eaten for breakfast. Two pop tarts, a glass of milk, and a half of cup of leftover spaghetti. (Don't ask)

Now, not only is our car covered in puke, but now my father is too.

Needless to say, we didn't get very far on the first day of our move.

I guess being in a family can be pretty messy sometimes.

Miss Little

Dear Journal,

I went to my classroom today. Mrs. McGee told me that I have one of the best rooms in the entire school. She said that the only downfall is that it is located in a separate hallway away from other classrooms.

It used to be the music room. Mrs. McGee began to tell me that the music program at E.R. Anderson grew so much, they had to build a brand new music room onto another area of the school building just to fit everyone. So, that left the old music room available to be a classroom.

The music room had everything. Not only did I have a traditional classroom, but there were two mini rooms that connected to the larger room. They were once soundproof rooms, where students could practice playing their instruments and not distract the rest of the classroom.

I decided to convert the sound proof rooms to cute study buddy areas so that students that needed to work together on small group projects could in a smaller space.

Who would've thought that I would need the study buddy rooms for something else?

Stuart

It's not easy being the middle child. I have two older brothers Max and Mark and two younger sisters Lily and Rose. I also have a pet hamster named Genevieve and she is by far my favorite family member. My two older brothers are twins and are pretty much the best of friends. We don't really do anything together even though they are only two years older than me. They are "fifth graders" and "fifth graders" are too cool to hang out with "third graders." That's why I like playing pranks on them. That way they notice me.

Lily is five and Rose is three. Lily is obsessed with her baby dolls. All sixteen of them. And they each have VERY interesting names. Seriously, everyone in the family knows them. We have to because they join us for dinner every night.

There's Watermelonandrea.

Cupcakes

Princess Only One Eyeball

Baby Foot Keeps Popping Off

Sir Phillip

Little Neil

Thumb Sucker Baby

And I could probably keep going, but I'm sure you want to move on. See how annoying little sisters can be. Baby dolls. Ick!

Mom says Lily's baby dolls helps enhance her imagination.

She talks to imaginary animals and inanimate objects. I think her imagination is just fine, Mom.

So see, even in a house filled with five kids. I have no one.

Sometimes, being part of a big family can be rather lonely.

Paz

School starts in two weeks, so Uncle G decides to take me shopping. I'm really a simple kid. A couple pairs of shorts, some t-shirts, and pair of sneakers and I'm just fine.

Uncle G wants only the best for me.

And simple is just not a word in his vocabulary.

So, we head to the name brand store and G buys me everything in sight. Shorts, jeans, sneakers, polos. I'm pretty sure he even put a mannequin head in one of the bags. His arms are loaded with bags of clothes and I'm practically dragging two bags across the mall floor.

"Are you sure this will be enough?" he asks me.

I shake my head.

"Yes G," I tell him. "I have way more than I need."

"Good, kid." he replies. "You deserve everything...and more."

I don't know where I'd be without Uncle G.

Sometimes families are the best gift you could ever receive.

Harper

There are only three days until school starts.

       That's thirty-six hours.
       2,160 minutes
       129,600 seconds 129,599... 129,598...

Well you get the idea.

I seriously cannot wait.

    I love school. I love school almost as much as I love rainbow unicorns and I love unicorns A LOT! I also love glitter and the color purple. You know what, now that I have your attention I'm going to tell you everything you need to know about me.

       My name is Harper Grace Meadows.
         I'm eight years old.
         I love school.
         I love reading books.
         I enjoy learning math facts and solving math problems.

I don't however, enjoy brussels sprouts or hummus. Sorry mom, but brussel sprouts smell funny and I prefer dipping my carrot sticks in ranch dip. Thank you very much.

I love unicorns.

I really *love* unicorns.

I have a dog named Buster and he is my best friend. Mom calls him my "dog brother." She says that Buster is the closest thing that I'll get to a sibling, because I keep her plenty busy.

My mom is a great mom! She tucks me in at night and she makes me peanut butter banana smoothies for breakfast. Sometimes she puts in chocolate chips for "funsy." See? I told you she was the best.

There is one thing about my life that is not all sunshine and rainbows. I don't like to talk about it much, because it makes my mom really sad.

I'm sick. Like really sick! I have something called Cystic Fibrosis. It basically means that there is this icky stuff on my lungs that makes it hard for me to breath. That makes it hard for me to do some things that I see my friends do. I can't ride horses or spend time in the barn. The doctors tell me that if I breath that stuff in, it could make it even harder for me to breath. So, even if unicorns did exist. I wouldn't be able to ride them.

But there is one place I can ride them.

Right, smack dab in the middle of my imagination.

Miss Little

Dear Journal,

Can you believe school starts tomorrow? I get to meet my students tomorrow. I can't sleep. I'm so excited.

Wish me luck,

♥ Miss Little

Hope

Mom and Dad started fighting again. I'm trying to get ready to go to school, but I don't want to walk past their room. It's times like this, I wish the bathroom was closer to my room, that way I wouldn't have to go near their room when they are in the middle of an argument.

"You're never going to change!!" I hear Dad yell.

"Maybe I don't want to!" Mom retaliates.

Tears start to glide down my cheek, but I don't even notice. Their arguments have become a new normal and I'm just along for this roller coaster ride.

I finally find the courage to walk to the bathroom. I start to speed up as I edge closer to my parents' room. My heart starts skipping faster and just as I think I'm about to make it to bathroom without anyone noticing me I hear, "I just want out!" Dad was telling mom that he was done. He wanted out. He didn't want to stay.

My dad wanted to leave me? Was this a joke?

I ran into my parents' room and wrapped my arms around his waist.

"Dad," I pleaded, "Please don't leave me. I need you!"

Dad took me by the hand and walked me downstairs. He sat me on the couch. I thought he was getting ready to tell me that he wasn't going to leave. That he and mom just said some words that they didn't mean.

But he did the exact opposite.

He walked out the door and didn't even look back.

He left his seven-year-old daughter on the living room couch.

What a great way to start off the brand-new school year.

Stuart

It's the first day of school tomorrow. How fantastic...not. Max and Mark are excited about school because they are starting middle school and they tell me that the girls in middle school are "so cute." Yuck! I'm pretty sure that girls have cooties.

One time, a girl named Maggie, high fived me in the first grade and I was so sure my hand was going to fall off.

I never touched a girl again.

I don't want cooties.

You know how I told you earlier that I love to play pranks on my brothers. Well. what better time to play a prank than on the first day of school. Max and Mark both have sweet tooths. They also are both terrified of cafeteria food. I don't know why though. The cafeteria makes the best french toast sticks in the entire world.

My mom packs their lunch the night before school. She draws cute little notes and pictures on the paper sack and stores them on the same shelf in the fridge every time. It's so predictable. As quietly as I can, I open the paper bags and pull out the baggie of chocolate sandwich cookies. (You know the really good ones. Mega double stuffed)

Before anyone notices I take two cookies out from each baggie and twist off the top sandwich cookie. (I did mention they have a sweet tooth, right?) I then put a drop or six of black food coloring on the white and delicious filling.

P.S. I snuck into Mom's baking pantry and found the expensive food coloring that she only uses when decorating our birthday cakes.

I put the lids back on the cookies without anyone even noticing. Just as I was about to open the fridge door to complete the final task of my mission (putting the cookies back in the boys' lunch bag) Lily comes into the kitchen.

"Stuey," she whines, "Can I pwease have a cookie?"

I have to think of something fast. I can't give her one of the cookies in my hand, then everyone will know what I have done and this prank was meant for my older brothers, not my little sister.

"I tell you what," I say to her, "How about we play hide and seek and then after, I'll get you a cookie."

Phew. Before I could even begin to start counting, Lil was already running away. I put the cookies back in their lunch boxes and went to my room.

It wasn't until I was getting ready for bed that I remembered I was supposed to find Lily. I sure hope someone else did.

Miss Little

Dear Journal,

It's 2:30 in the morning and I know I should be sleeping, but I can't. I'm so nervous and excited. In just six hours I will officially be a teacher. I will have students sitting at desks in a classroom that I decorated with cute little signs and inspirational banners. I will meet them at the door. I will give handshakes and hugs. All my dreams are about to come true.

How can one sleep at a time like this?

Love,
Miss Little

Jillie

"Happy First Day of School," Dad says as he knocks on my bedroom door. "Rise and shine, my beautiful girl."

I try to act like I'm not excited at all, but the truth is, in some sick way, I can't wait to go to my new school. There wasn't a lot to do around here since we didn't have a pool close by. I quickly got dressed in an outfit my mom and I had picked out last night. It was nice to chat with my mom, because since she started her new job, I don't see her as much anymore. I'm not entirely sure what she does, but whatever it is, it must be important, because she is always at work.

"Good luck at work today, Annie." Dad tells her. I'm pretty sure they kiss after that, but I always close my eyes before they do that. Gross.

Dad secures Carson in his carseat as I buckle myself in. He tells me that once he starts his new job and Carson goes to nursery school, that I will have to ride the bus. He also informs me that the bus ride could be longer than an hour, so I should probably find some good books at the library. I never had to ride the bus in Texas. We could walk to school from our apartment. Mom and

Carson would always walk with me because Mom said it was good exercise. Now, I have to ride the bus alone? I don't like it. Not one bit.

The van begins to roll backwards and a tear falls from my face. So much for being excited an hour ago. My happiness had quickly turned to fear. Fear of something new. Fear of not being liked at school. Fear of having an awful teacher. Fear of not having friends. The list could have gone on and on.

I was almost getting ready to have a full-blown meltdown with giant crocodile tears, but out of the corner of my eye, I saw something that would soon change my whole world forever.

The cutest dog I had ever seen in my entire life.

Paisley

Oh, it really was a cold one last night. I ended up sleeping underneath the porch of a nice family's house. I don't think they had a dog, because I'm pretty sure if they did, it would've noticed I was there and probably barked up a storm.

I'm glad they didn't have a dog.

I had the best night's sleep that I've had in a very long time. Not since I was "home." I heard a young girl's laugh coming from inside the house and it made me miss my old life. The life I had when I would get belly rubs and warm soapy baths. I hated baths at the time, but I could really use one right now.

I waited until I heard everyone leave the house before I crawled out from underneath the porch. I took off in the opposite direction of the white minivan and I was pretty certain that they wouldn't notice me. It wasn't until a few roads later that our paths would cross.

In the backseat of that white minivan I looked into the eyes of one of the saddest little girls I had ever seen and I knew that I had to follow her. I needed to make sure she was okay.

Harper

I am now a third grader and now that I have your attention, I need to tell you a few things.

First of all, I had to make sure I was wearing the perfect outfit for the very first day of school. (In case you were wondering, I'm wearing a beautiful unicorn dress with sparkly rainbow shoes. Mom says I look magical).

Second of all, I also have to tell you that I have a brand-new teacher. Her name is Miss Little. She's not Mrs. Little or Ms. Little, but Miss Little. Remember that.

Lastly, my lungs are not doing as well as they should be doing. It's harder to breath and I have a "special treatment" at school now. I've never had to do that before and it makes me so nervous. I don't want the kids to think I'm weird because I have to spend a half hour at the nurse's office every day.

This stinks.

Paz

Uncle G gave me a fist bump and then I walked on the bus. I wasn't nervous at all, not even a little. School is the place where I know people love me. Now, I know that Uncle G loves me, but he's only one person. At school, so many people love me.

Last year, I spent many afternoons talking to Mrs. Pratt, our gym teacher. Mrs. Pratt would just let me talk. If I was sad, I could cry and she would hug me and tell me I would be okay. She told me that I was strong and smart and brave. She also told me that everyone at this school would help me. They would make sure that I became my best self. I didn't know at the time, but the someone that would change my life and bring out the absolute best in me, had four legs and a wet nose.

Stuart

On the bus ride into school I could only think about my brothers and their charcoal smiles. Oh, how I wish I could be there to see it, but I'm sure it's only a matter of time before I hear about it. I can't wait to find out how they embarrassed themselves in front of all the "cute" girls. Ha.

The bus pulls into the school parking lot and my heart sinks. Summer vacation is really over. Bummer. I step off the bus and before I could even walk toward the school doors, I noticed something odd in the distance. But it's really not something. It's someone and we are about to meet that someone. Soon.

Miss Little

I can barely contain my enthusiasm as the children start entering my classroom. I hear laughter in the hallways and I see smiles in my classroom and the children spot the present wrapped at their desk. I tell them they can't open them yet, but that doesn't keep them from smiling.

"Okay children, please find your seats," I tell them in my sweetest voice. They are a bit rambunctious, but I don't mind. My next set of directions is a bit boring; pick your lunch choice, find your book box, meet your study buddy. Before I know it, the morning is over and it's time for recess. Little do I know, that when recess is over, I will be introduced to a new student.

Stuart

Okay. So, I have to tell you. I was really *really* not looking forward to coming back to school, but I have to confess, I think my teacher is kind of "cool." She gave us a present. I'm not sure what it is yet, because she told us not to open it. We had a pretty fun morning. She told us that we would have special "buddies" that we could work with on projects and stuff. Mine is a kid named Paz. He's pretty cool. He's quiet, but cool.

Miss Little told us it was time for recess, so we all quickly got in line. I mean, we just cannot waste any time outside on the playground. I have slides to slide down, swings to swing on, and monkey bars to, well you get the picture. Miss Little even complimented us on how quiet and respectful we were. I beamed a little with pride. I have never been complimented on the first day of school before. I usually try to prank the teacher on the first day of school. Last year, I gave my first-grade teacher, Ms. Donaldson, a chocolate covered onion that looked just like a gourmet chocolate apple. The face she made was priceless. I'm pretty sure I even made her puke.

Miss Little was different though. She gave me a present and I have a feeling if I made her puke, she'd take my present away.

Harper

I didn't go outside for recess. I walked to the door and I was going to go outside, but then I started to feel icky. Cystic Fibrosis really stinks sometimes. I think Miss Little could tell I was bummed out. She told me I could spend some time with her in the classroom and we could play a board game if I wanted to. I wanted to.

"I just have to run to the office to make a few copies," she told me as the final student walked outside, "would you like to come with me? I could really use your help."

There's one more thing you don't know about me. I am extremely helpful. I once helped my mom organize her underwear drawer by color. Let me just tell you, that was NOT the best job. It was extremely awkward and uncomfortable. I thought about telling Miss Little that story, but I didn't want to scare her on the first day.

On our walk to the office, I noticed something out the hallway window. There is a giant window near the front entrance of our school. Miss Little told me that it was probably just a kid and I shouldn't worry about it. I couldn't help but question it. It didn't look like a kid.
It looked like a dog.

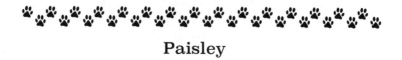

Paisley

When I had a family, there was a little girl and a little boy. The girl was Kenzie and the boy was Walter. The girl was older and the boy was little, but they were both mine. Kenzie liked to take me on walks and Walter would sneak me cookies every chance he could get.

Those kids were amazing.

My life changed this morning when I went for my morning walk and I saw them. Children, not Kenzie and Walter, but children that reminded me of them. Watching the children getting on the bus reminded me of Kenzie's first day of Kindergarten and she was so excited. And the time Walter had to get a new backpack even though he wasn't going to school. I wanted to watch that bus for hours because it reminded me of my old home. I tried to hide behind the oak tree so they couldn't see me. But I saw them. I saw their smiles. I heard their laughs.

I began to whine. Not because I was hungry, or tired, or cold. I was lonely. I missed my family and I didn't understand why I didn't have one anymore.

Jillie

The recess whistle sounded three times and everyone lined up quickly. I was so shocked, because no one had to say a word, but the kids knew exactly what to do. Miss Little met us at the door and she told us that once we got back to our classroom, we could open our present. I was so excited. I couldn't wait to unwrap my gift.

One of the students asked if we could walk around the school for a few minutes and enter through a different door. I really wanted this to happen so I could tour the entire building. I kind of expected Miss Little to say no. She even had that no expression on her face. I know that expression, because my mom looks like that every time I ask to trade Carson in for a different model.

"Sure," she said, "we just have to walk quickly. There are a lot of memories we still have to make today."

So, there we were. Fifteen third graders walking down the sidewalk. We were all too busy watching Miss Little to notice, that behind our line, walked a beautiful dog. The soon to be sixteenth student.

Paisley

Man, these kids can really walk and are so quiet. I wonder how long it will take for them to notice I'm behind them?

Miss Little

They don't really tell you everything you need to know in teacher school (also known as college).

I know how to create lesson plans.

I know how important reading aloud to children is.

I know that students learn better when they can play.

But what I don't know. What do you do when a dog enters your classroom and wants to learn too?

Paz

I've never had a dog. Or a fish. Or a cat.

Uncle G told me that once I got a little bit older, we could get a dog. He says that dogs are a lot of work. One time, he told me that he had a dog growing up that chewed everything in sight. The dog once ate a leg off of a table. His mom was not happy about that at all.

I still think dogs are cool though. I mean have you read *Because of Winn-Dixie?*

So, there I was, walking in line outside, minding my own business, with my hands at my side and my eyes looking right in front. When I heard something behind me. I was scared. A little too scared. What if I looked behind me and a skunk was about to spray me? What if I turned around there was baby bear, or a mongoose, or a crazy squirrel? (Hey, don't question me. I've read books. Squirrels are crazy.)

I knew we were almost to the entrance of our school, so I turned around. I was preparing myself for screaming, "RUN!"

I turned my head. I first noticed her floppy ears. She had the face of a beagle with her long, floppy ears. I then noticed her fur. It was brown and white and tan. She even had white patches on her head. She was so adorable. I just wanted to run over and pet her. But as I lunged forward to pet her, she took off. She ran away faster than any dog I've ever seen.

I shouted," Wait. Stop!" and when I did the whole entire class looked back and they all saw what I did.
The most beautiful dog in the world.

Stuart

Okay. Can this day get any better? Not only would my brothers have black teeth, but there was a dog at school. An actual dog. It was even walking behind us in line. How crazy is that?

We were waiting to open the entrance door. I have to tell you that yours truly, me Stuart Ryan Murphy, was Tour Guide. That means that I walk first in line. I make sure the line is ready for the hallway. It is a great responsibility. So, our line is looking amazing. We are all walking quietly and I can tell that Miss Little is proud. When all of the sudden someone yells, "Stop." and the whole class starts screaming, "Dog. There's a dog. Hey, you see that dog?"

Those kids were so out of control that Miss Little had to take over.

Miss Little

Things they really don't teach you at teacher school.

- How do you manage a classroom of fifteen students that are extremely worried about a puppy that just visited their school?

- How do you control their questions and calm their fears?

- How do you help the dog that they can't stop talking about?

Harper

When we all got back to our classroom, we were too worried about the dog to do anything else. Miss Little even had a fun activity that involved bubble gum and noodles, but we were too preoccupied with the pooch to even wonder about the unusual food combination.

"Miss Little," Paz asked, "What do you think happened to that dog?"

I could tell Miss Little was hesitant to answer the question. I don't think she wanted us to worry, but we couldn't help it. We wanted to know what was going on with the dog. Why was it here and why did it run away from us so fast?

Miss Little could've told us that we shouldn't worry about it. That the dog was probably fine and just temporarily ran away from home or got separated from the owner, but she didn't. She thanked us for showing compassion and caring for someone else. She told us that after school, she'd walk around and see if she could find the dog and she would let us know what she found out. She even let us create Lost Dog posters that she could pass out to the public.

I was beginning to really like Miss Little.

Stuart

Alright. Confession time. I have never said this in my entire life. Not once. Not ever. But today, I didn't hate school. In fact, I almost liked it a little, but please don't tell anyone.

I saw a dog at school. I saw a *cute* dog at school.

After I saw that adorable little dog, I kind of figured that this school year, may be different from all the others.

After the dog spotting, Miss Little took us back to the classroom and we created *Lost Dog Posters*. We were so caught up in making sure that dog had a home, that we forgot about unwrapping the presents Miss Little bought us. She told us that it was okay, that we could unwrap our presents tomorrow.

Miss Little also gave us our first homework assignment as third graders, but it wasn't the horrible kind of homework. She wanted us to write a letter to the dog that was lost. What kinds of things would we need to say to the dog to make him or her stay and not run away? What questions could we ask to know what happened to him or her and how we could help?

I hate to admit this, but I was actually looking forward to this homework assignment.

Harper

Mom picked me up from school today, because I had a doctor's appointment right after. I should be used to going to the doctors, but I'm really not. They still make me extremely nervous. My hands start to sweat and my heart starts to beat faster. She tells me that everything will be just fine. I think she says that to calm herself down too!

We are almost to the doctor's office, when I notice the tears streaming down Mom's face.

"It's times like now, I wish your father was still around." And just like that I wasn't worried about going to the doctors, I was worried about my mom.

Miss Little

Dear Journal,

My first day of school went nothing like what I imagined it would. In my wildest dreams, I never would have thought I'd be teaching my students about the great responsibility that comes with owning a pet, how sometimes those pets run away from home and can't find their way back. We talked about what we can do to be good citizens for everyone; stray or runaway dogs included. I even came up with a last-minute homework assignment to write letters to the dog we saw when we were walking in from the playground. I told them we could read them aloud tomorrow and maybe the canine would come visit.

So, imagine my surprise when I was driving home tonight and spotted that little dog. She wasn't a very big dog, but I saw her. She was walking down by the post office almost to the only grocery store in town. I decided to pull my car over and just as I did, my favorite song came on the radio and Brad Paisley was singing it.

I didn't even mean to say it. I just blurted it out. I opened the car door and yelled out, "Paisley!"

And she came running. Her floppy ears were waving in the wind and her little legs were running as fast as she could. My car door was still open and she jumped right inside.

I don't know why it happened and I still don't know how it happened.

But it happened.

Paisley

I memorized her voice. I knew the gentle way she talked to her students and how much she loved them, just by the way she spoke. I could've stayed in that line forever with her and the children, but something didn't quite feel right, so I ran. I took off to the bakery in town. They sometimes put old bread out for the ducks to eat, but sometimes if I time it right, I can have some too.

I didn't make it to the bakery. I wasn't even close to the bakery, when I heard her voice again. She called me Paisley and I liked it. I liked her. So, I ran as fast as I could and I jumped in the car she was driving and I sat right there on the front seat.

Wherever she was going, I wanted to go too.

Stuart

Well, that didn't go quite the way I wanted. Apparently, Max could tell I put black food coloring in the cookie, so he saved it and gave it to Lily when he got home. Lily was quite upset at her newly blackened mouth, so Mom yelled at Max. Max of course, blamed me for the entire incident (even though I meant it to be for him and *not* Lily). Mom told me that she and Dad were going to have a long talk with me as soon as he got home.

Fantastic.

I decided that while I was waiting to get spoken to, I might as well make myself useful and do my homework assignment. At least, I could possibly help someone else out, even if I was miserable.

Lily

Hi. I'm Lily. I'm five. I like baby dolls and I don't like avocados. Those things make me gag.

I also really don't like having black teeth. I just wanted a chocolate cookie before dinner. I know Mom doesn't like me to eat sweets before dinner, but I needed that cookie. I didn't need black teeth.

Thanks, Max.

Stuart

So, there I am in my room, writing a letter to a dog, when I hear Dad's truck pull into the driveway. I should be used to having chats like this. The day Officer Morris showed up, Dad and I had a long chat. I know I haven't told you about that story yet, but I will, I promise.

I hear Rose start to cry and Lily runs up to my room. She knocks on my door.

"Stuey?" she asks, "Can I come in?"

I wanted to tell her no, but I said yes. She walks in with Watermelonandrea in her hand. Her mouth is still black and I can tell she's been crying. She asks what I'm doing, but I don't want to tell her. I just tell her that I'm doing a homework assignment and when she's older she will have to do homework too!

I start to feel guilty as she tells me how upset she is that Max turned her mouth black. I should tell her the truth, that I'm the one who put the black food coloring in the cookie, but I don't. I just let her think that it was all Max and I'm completely innocent.

I hear someone come up the stairs and I assume it's
Dad. Lily must've thought the same thing because she goes
running to find him. I can hear him tell her how much he
missed her and how much he loves her.

Gee. He never tells me that.

I hear two knocks on my door and Dad walks in. He
looks tired, but he doesn't look mad.

"Stuart?" He asks, "Want to tell me what happened
today and why your mother wants to send you to military
school?"

I should tell him the truth, but I don't say anything. I
just continue creating my letter to the dog.

"Stuart?"

I can tell by the tone in his voice that he is
disappointed. I never like to disappoint my dad, but
sometimes even in this big family, I feel like I'm the only
one who cares about me. Dad's working all the time,
Mom's busy doing mom-things, Max and Mark have each
other and Lily and Rose are practically best friends.

That leaves me, Stuart, all by himself.

Miss Little

There is a dog in my car. I'm not exactly sure what to do with it. I could take him home, but I'm not sure if I'm supposed to have a dog in my little house. I could take it to an animal shelter, but I'm not sure my heart could handle that. I could drive around and see if anyone is out looking for a lost dog.

Before I could do anything, I had to get this dog something to eat. She looked hungry. I could see some of her rib bones and knew she needed a decent meal. The closest pet shop was over forty minutes away, but I knew what I had to do. I started to drive.

Paisley looked comfortable in the passenger seat. She curled up and started to fall asleep. I put my hand on the top of her head and began softly petting her beautiful fur. I had to admit, she was the sweetest dog I think I'd ever met.

By the time, I reached the pet store, Paisley had to go to the bathroom. We took a short walk

around the outside of the building before we went inside. I could tell she was excited. When we walked in the door, I could tell Paisley had been here before. She knew exactly where to go to get a treat.

I held Paisley the entire time, since I didn't have a leash or a collar. We soon found an adorable purple collar with yellow paisley and a matching leash. It wasn't long before I noticed a matching purple dog bed and knew she had to have that too! By the time I bought dog food, dog treats, flea medicine, and dog shampoo, I had almost spent my first paycheck.

But that's okay. I had a new friend.

Jillie

Day Two.

Dad tells me this morning that he can't drop me off. Carson caught some disgusting illness and he has to take him to the doctor. Mom had gone to work early, so the only way I could go to school was to ride the dreaded school bus.

I quickly got dressed and went downstairs. Mom had left a note next to my lunch:

"Sorry Jillie, this is all I could pack for your lunch. I promise I'll go grocery shopping tomorrow. Love, Mom"

I didn't even want to look inside.

This would've never happened in Texas.

The bus was three minutes early, so I ran out of the house as quick as I could. It wasn't until we were almost at school that I realized that I had my lunch box, but not my backpack with my homework.

What an amazing third grader I am.

Paz

When I walked into school today, something felt different, but I couldn't tell what is was. Miss Little met us out by the front doors yesterday, but today she was nowhere to be found. I also didn't see anyone from my class and started to get a little worried.

I walked down the hallway and turned by the water fountain. Since our room was on the other side of the school, the walk to the classroom was kind of creepy. There wasn't anyone around me as I walked down the music room hallway. It was so eerie when I heard what sounded like a dog bark and I couldn't help but think of the letter that I wrote to the dog yesterday.

Was I hearing things?

Miss Little

Dear Journal,

Yes, I know what you're thinking. I could lose my job if someone knew I purposefully brought a dog to school without permission, but I couldn't leave her at home. Believe me, I tried.

She whined when I left. She cried louder when I stepped off the front porch. When I opened my car door, I heard her howl. When I started my car, she did a mixture of barking, whining, and howling. I couldn't leave her alone and I couldn't miss work.

So, I did the only logical thing.
I brought her to work with me.

Wish me luck.
Miss Little

Harper

I wasn't expecting to walk into my classroom and have Miss Little meet with us in the sound proof room.

"Come in children," she told us, "as quietly as you can."

I knew she had a secret, but I wasn't sure what it was.

She told us to find our letters and sit criss cross applesauce in a circle on the floor. So we all did, as quickly as we could.

She began to tell us about the importance of helping others and she asked if anyone wanted to share their letters. I raised my hand as fast as I could.

Miss Little told me to go ahead and share my intelligence with the world.

Dear Playground Puppy,

I'm not sure why you took off yesterday, but I want you to know that I love dogs. I have a dog at home named Buster and I love him. In fact, he's practically my brother. I was just wondering why you took off yesterday? Where did you go? Are you okay?

Do you have a family? If you don't I could ask my mom if you can come live with us. I'm sure she wouldn't mind.

Love,
Harper Grace

Stuart

Miss Little asked me to read my letter next. I'm pretty sure I heard a dog bark when Harper was reading hers, but I think it could've just been wishful thinking. Dad once told Mom that having a dog would be good for me and we should consider it, but Mom said no. She had too much to do without having an animal in the house.

I cleared my throat and started to read.

> *"Dear Four Legs,*
>
> *My name is Stuart. I am eight and I like dinosaurs, sticking my tongue out, and eating cookies. I also enjoy playing tricks on people; especially my brothers.*
>
> *I wish you could come back. I could use someone like you to talk to.*
>
> *If you don't have a family, you can borrow mine. Just know, you may want to return them.*
>
> *Your friend,*
>
> *Stuart"*

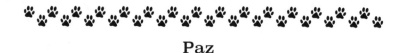

Paz

So, there I am in our sound proof room, when Stuart read his letter out loud. He drew a really nice picture that he showed to the class too. I wasn't expecting what happened next. Miss Little told us that she had a big secret. This secret was so big that if anyone outside our class found out, she could lose her job.

I wasn't sure I liked the sound of this.

Miss Little told us about her trip home last night. How she was driving her car when she spotted the same dog that we saw earlier in the day. It sounded a little bit rehearsed, but I went along with the story.

We all waited quietly as Miss Little went back to the classroom and came back with a wrapped up purple towel. The towel was moving. Miss Little told us that we weren't allowed to say a thing when we saw what was in the towel. We weren't allowed to freak out or scream or laugh.

I couldn't believe what I saw. Miss Little was holding the dog from yesterday. Even though Miss Little told us not to scream, Harper started screaming and crying. Sometimes, girls can be so dramatic.

So, there I am trying not to freak out and become an emotional basket case, when the cute little puppy makes her way over to me. I melt into a giant puddle of Paz, because this puppy is just so adorable. She even starts licking my face and I can't help but giggle.

"What's her name?" Harper asks while wiping the tears from her eyes. I start petting the dog's head and hold her tight in my lap. She doesn't even try to squirm away.

"Her name is Paisley," Miss Little answers.

Paisley looks up at Miss Little as soon as she said her name. Miss Little asked us to sit in a circle and we all did, even Paisley. She sat in between Jillie and I. The whole time.

Miss Little explained that Paisley would only be joining us today because we are breaking, as Miss Little puts it, "so many rules."

We stayed in the soundproof room for much of the morning, but then Paisley had to go to the bathroom. Just so you know, Paisley was not toilet trained. So, during recess, Miss Little had to sneak Paisley outside to go potty. Everything was going well, until Mr. Franklyn, another third-grade teacher, met us outside near the playground.

"A beautiful day, isn't it?" He asks, Miss Little. Miss Little, at the time, was holding a squirmy bag, trying to play it cool.

At this time, Harper senses what's going on and walks over to Mr. Franklyn.

"Mr. Franklyn," Harper says, "I think the playground slide is broken. Will you make sure it's safe for me?"

Harper and Mr. Franklyn walk over to the slide and Miss Little and a few of us go over to help keep Paisley hidden while she goes potty. Lucky for us, Harper was entertaining most everyone on the playground. She was channeling her inner Taylor Swift and was showing the whole playground her dance moves.

(I have to admit it, I was impressed.)

I looked over at Miss Little and she looked extremely stressed out. I could tell that Paisley really wanted to go for a walk, but Miss Little had to put her back into the bag she carried her in. The minute Miss Little put Paisley in the bag, the dog started to whine.

(And not very quietly I might add.)

Miss Little blew her whistle three times, even though we have fifteen minutes left of recess. Everyone lined up and we didn't even ask about it. Paisley continued to whine in the bag, but I wasn't that worried about it. Miss Little told us that we could chat with each other so that no one would be able to hear the unhappy dog.

Everything was going well. We were almost to the door of our classroom, when something drastic happened. Something we weren't expecting. Someone that could ruin our entire day. Our entire year.

Our principal, Mrs. McGee was standing in front of our classroom.

Mrs. Darcy McGee

The first time I met Miss Little I saw such great potential. She had such a passion for education and I could tell that she'd be an excellent addition to our elementary school. I saw that same passion when I saw her interacting with her students today.

I decided to pay her and her class a visit. I knew they were at recess, but I wanted to make sure I had enough time to check out the room and have a brief chat with Miss Little about her first few days.

I was a little surprised to hear how chatty Miss Little's class was as they walked into the building. I almost wanted to say something to Miss Little, but decided that I wouldn't this time, but if I heard them again later in the week, I would. The minute the children saw me, they stopped talking, and they looked at me as if they had seen a ghost.

I was staring back at 15 expressionless faces. They all just stood there, like frozen little statutes.

"Good Afternoon, children!" I said in my most upbeat and positive voice.

Miss Little directed her students to say, "Good Afternoon, Mrs. McGee."

It was quite lovely.

I asked Miss Little if it was a great time to visit, but just as she was about to answer a voiced called out from the back of the line.

"Miss Little. I don't feel so good."

I didn't recognize the voice, so I knew it had to be one of our new friends.

Miss Little responded back, "Oh no, Jillie. What's wrong?"

The sweet girl now walked closer to me. If she was sick, I did not want to be close to her. I love children, but I hate catching those crazy viruses.

The little girl started to cry.

"My stomach hurts so bad.....I think I might throw up."

Miss Little looked like she had her hands full, so I volunteered to walk Jillie to the nurse.

I'll be back to visit your class tomorrow, Miss Little.

Jillie

My acting skills are impeccable. Ever since the pukemobile incident, I've become very good at getting out unpleasant situations. I just pretend to be sick. When I saw Mrs. McGee by our door, I knew I had to get rid of her. I couldn't let Miss Little get into trouble. I couldn't let Mrs. McGee find Paisley. I needed to create a diversion that would focus the attention off of Miss Little and our class.

So I pretended to be sick. No matter what they tell you, most adults are scared of the stomach bug. They get all queasy and anxious and sometimes they even start gagging too! It's actually quite hilarious.

I did what I had to do.

From the moment I mentioned feeling ill, I noticed an immediate change in Mrs. McGee. She got all nervous and sweaty. I knew she wouldn't be staying for very long. She even volunteered to take me to the nurse's office.

Checkmate.

Paisley

Things that I like

1. Getting my belly rubbed
2. Those dog treats with the stuff in the middle
3. Car rides
4. My ears getting scratched
5. Squeaky toys
6. Children

What I don't like
1. Being left alone
2. Being abandoned
3. Being carried in a teacher's bag
4. Not having privacy when I have to go to the bathroom

But I do have to say, I'm kind of enjoying this whole, "going to school" thing. It's pretty awesome.

Hope

It's dark outside. Scary dark. Mom's working late again and I'm not sure when she'll be home. She left a peanut butter and jelly sandwich on the counter for me and a note to make sure my homework was done before I went to bed. I tried hard to be brave and not be scared, but the wind howling outside did not help at all.

I made sure all the doors were locked. After Dad left, we had to move into a small apartment. I missed my house. My street. My neighborhood. I even missed Mrs. McClintock from across the street who used to babysit me and made me go to bed at 7:30, so she could watch the "Hunk of Her Dreams" on *Jeopardy.*

I missed my old life.

Thanks Dad for ruining it.

I crawled into my bed and tried to fall asleep, but my racing heart was keeping me up. I needed my mom to come home. I needed a friend. I needed someone, anyone, to tell me that I was going to be alright.

But come to think of it, I'm not sure I'd even believe them. I don't think I'll be okay. Ever. Again.

Miss Little

I can never do what I did yesterday again. Bringing a dog school. How crazy is that? I love my job. I love my students and I can't do anything to jeopardize them again.

Not ever.

Paisley and I arrived home and I scratched her belly, I told her how thankful I was that she was a good girl at school. She was so great with the children. She was so kind to them. She sat with them as they read stories. They practiced their math facts with her and I'm so thankful that Jillie was able to come up with a plan on the spot like that.

But, I cannot have another day that like.

Or can I?

Paisley

I start to bark the minute I see the sun. I'm sure Miss Little is not happy with me, but when I was living on the streets, as soon as the sun came up, that's when I needed to start my day. I scratch at the front door a few times and start to dance around (because I really have to go to the bathroom) when I hear Miss Little come down the stairs.

I was really starting to like that girl.

She says," Good Morning," in a very sweet voice, clicks my leash to my collar, and starts walking outside. We walked around the front yard where there is a beautiful apple tree and the grass was so soft against my feet. I felt at home. I was home.

Miss Little began talking about all the things I could do at home today. She said that I could curl up on my dog bed and take a nap. I could play with Mr. Squeakers, my new stuffed moose. She told me that I could even lay on top of her bed if I started missing her.

Wait. Was she leaving me home today? Was she going to school and making me stay here by myself?

I don't think so.

Jillie

I probably shouldn't write right now. Dad forgot to get me up, because he was up all night with Carson. Apparently, his puking is not limited to automobiles. Dad woke me up five minutes before the bus was set to arrive and expected me to get ready in that amount of time.

I love my dad, but sometimes he just doesn't understand women.

Since we were new in the area, Dad didn't feel comfortable leaving Carson with one of the neighbors. He also knew how Carson was with vomiting in his car. I'm pretty sure I heard him say that the day Carson and I puked in the car was one of the "worst days of his life."

Gee whiz.

Dad called Mom in a panic. She told Dad that she would take me to school during her "coffee" run which would mean I would be an hour late to school. This never would've happened to me in Texas.

Paz

I told Uncle G about the dog visiting our school when we were waiting for the morning bus. He smiled. He said that I must have a pretty crazy teacher to sneak a dog into our school.

She may be crazy, but I think she's pretty wonderful.

Uncle G handed me my lunch bag when he saw the bus turn its yellow lights on. I asked Uncle G if he rode the bus when he was my age, but he didn't answer. I don't think he likes talking about his childhood, because he misses his younger years. That's when his sister, my mom, was alive.

"Have a great day at school, Kid," he tells me. I wave as the bus drives away and his body gets smaller and smaller in the distance. I wave until I can't see him anymore.

"Is that your dad?" a fourth grader asks me. I really want to tell him yes. It's pretty normal for dads to drop their children off at bus stops.

Instead I decide to tell the truth.

"That's my Uncle G," I reply.

The fourth grader looks puzzled and I have a feeling I know where this conversation is going to go.

"You live with your uncle?" He continues to look confused.

"I do."

"Why?"

"He's my family."

I could tell that this fourth grader wasn't the sharpest tool in the shed. I also didn't want to go into detail about my family story.

Mostly, because there wasn't much to tell.

My mom died. The only family member I have is my Uncle G.

Luckily, we pulled into the school parking lot before the kid had the opportunity to ask me any more questions.

And even though he stopped asking questions, I still did.

Who was my mom? What did she do? What was her favorite color? Her favorite candy? What was she like as a kid? Was she quiet like me or was she more outgoing like Uncle G? But most of all, I want to know why she isn't here with me. Today.

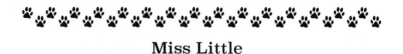

Miss Little

The students are bursting with excitement as they enter my classroom. I can see their smiling faces. I ask them to complete the morning routine. Choose their lunches, take attendance, sharpen their pencils. You know, all the fun morning things.

"Miss Little?" Harper asks, "Where's Paisley?"

I could tell all the students were thinking that same question, but I wasn't exactly sure how I was going to respond. I knew whatever I replied with would probably upset most of my class. So, I just told the truth.

"She had to stay home. Where she belongs."

A few girls started to cry. A few boys started to pout. I started to sweat.

"Teach on," I told myself. "You've got this!"

(Sometimes teachers have to give ourselves little pep talks to make it through the day.)

Fifteen minutes went by and I broke the students up into teams so we could review some basic math facts. (You know 2+9=11 and 3+7=10, that kind of thing.) I try to have my students warm up with math every morning. Sometimes, we play math games on the computers, sometimes we play math board games, and sometimes (like today) we play a shouting math activity.

I wasn't expecting Mrs. McGee to walk into the room.

"Good Morning, Miss Little," she says to me as I begin passing students' game boards out.

"What are we doing right now?" she asks.

My hands started to tremble. It wasn't that I was doing anything wrong. This was the first time Mrs. McGee was watching me teach a lesson.

"We are just practicing our math fluency facts," I respond, trying to hide how nervous I am from her.

I can feel her eyes beam at me as I review the directions with the students. She anxiously awaits as

I pass out the math game board and delegate the rest of the jobs to the students. Mrs. McGee decides to play along with one group of students and my heart starts to smile. I immediately realize that Mrs. McGee is here to make sure my students are learning and growing and that I'm being the best third grade teacher I can be.

I know that I am almost in the clear. Mrs. McGee grabs her pen and her clipboard, when out through the back window, I notice something.

Rather someone.

Paisley

I love Miss Little. Dog Mom. Mom. Whatever you want to call her. I love her, but the fact that she left me home alone today did not make me a happy puppy.

In fact, I was rather miserable.

I whined for a solid ten minutes after she left. I can't tell time yet, but it felt like ten minutes or maybe twenty.

You know, I'm not sure anymore. I was traumatized being home alone. I like adventure and I like freedom.

But I also like people and I don't like being away from them.

I've been alone long enough.

I started to scratch at the front door, but it didn't open. That's the door that I'm the most familiar with. That's the door where Miss Little takes me outside and where she enters. I know that door well.

I also know that there is a back door, but I'm not sure where it is. I use my nose to try to smell outside, but I can't. I start to feel frustrated. I need to escape this house. I need to go find Miss Little, to find my friends, to be with everyone.

I jump up on the back of Miss Little's couch, when I notice something. I think I may have just found my way out.

Miss Little had left the window open just a crack. I start to bite down on the wood frame surrounding the window. It

77

starts to move a little. I push my nose through the crack and try to force the window to open further. At first, it doesn't move at all. It doesn't even budge. I start to whine. I just want to be with my family.

I lay down on the couch. I want to give up. It's hard and I'm tired. My eyes close and I start to picture my day yesterday. I imagine Miss Little teaching her students. I imagine Harper smiling and Stuart laughing. I realize that I need to figure out a way to get back to school.

I wasn't giving up this easy.

I put my nose as far as I can go through the crack in the window. With all my might, I push up and before I know it, the window is open enough for me to jump out of.

E.R. Anderson Elementary. Here I come.

Stuart

I had to be on my best behavior when Mrs. McGee showed up. Mrs. McGee is the boss of the school. She can make your life miserable. (Trust me, I know. Last year, I spent a lot of time with her.)

I almost blurted out a few times, but I caught myself and raised my hand. I saw Mrs. McGee smile and I started feeling pretty good about myself. I wasn't used to someone smiling at me. Usually everyone is looking pretty grouchy at me, especially after I prank them.

So, there we were playing our math game, when I saw Miss Little look out the window. I stared out the window too, because I was curious what was out there. I felt my mouth drop when I saw who it was.

Our class dog, Paisley.

I couldn't let Mrs. McGee see Paisley. I knew if she did, Miss Little would probably lose her job and I couldn't let that happen.

I ran out into the hallway and started running as fast as I could.

"Bet you can't catch me, Mrs. McGee!" I dared my principal. I ran far away from Miss Little's classroom. I knew that if I ran

to the 5th grade wing it would be the furthest away from Miss Little's class. I started to slow down just a little so I could make sure Mrs. McGee was chasing me. Right around the water fountain, I spotted her, so I continued to run.

"Get Paisley," was the only thought that crossed my mind. That was until the school's resource officer caught me by the fourth-grade wing.

Busted.

Harper

I honestly thought Stuart had lost his mind when he ran out of the room asking Mrs. McGee to chase him. I didn't realize that Paisley was just outside our classroom. I could tell Miss Little was surprised. She had that frazzled look on her face. I knew she was thinking, "What do I do?"

I knew what to do. Mom says I have leadership qualities. She says I get it from my dad. He was a Commander in the Navy and he knew how to handle situations like this.

"I've got her, Miss Little," I said as I walked toward the door. I didn't even ask permission. Sometimes you gotta do what you gotta do.

I opened the outside door of our school and before I could even call her name, Paisley came running. She's inside before I could even blink. Just then, I could tell that today was going to be a very interesting day.

Jillie

I honestly couldn't believe what had just happened. This never would've happened in Texas. Since I was late for school, I had walked down with Mrs. McGee. I couldn't believe how fast she was when Stuart dared her to chase him. School was never like this in Texas.

After Harper came in with Paisley, Miss Little called us into the soundproof room. I could tell she meant business, because she didn't even crack a smile. She held Paisley in her hands and began to talk to us.

"I don't know how Paisley managed to escape my house, but she did," she paused, clearing her throat as if she was trying to hold back tears. "I really think Paisley needs to be with us for whatever reason. I can get in big trouble for keeping her here, but I think she has a lot to teach us about community, compassion, and caring for each other. Are you okay if she stays?"

Everyone shouted out, "Yes!"

Well, almost everyone, Stuart was probably still running around school.

I think he just became our classroom hero.

Stuart

Okay. So, today was not how I wanted it to be. After Mr. Elementary Cop caught me, he took me to Mrs. McGee's office where she was already on the phone with my mom. (You know how last night ended right.) I was in deep deep trouble.

"Mrs. Murphy," I heard her say, "You will need to come pick up your son. He is suspended for the rest of the day. Stuart needs to know that his actions have consequences. I would like to speak with you and your husband soon."

This was not good. My mom was one thing, but the minute Dad got involved with anything I knew I was going down.

I knew Mom was saying something to Mrs. McGee, but I couldn't tell what. Mrs. McGee just kept shaking her head, like she was agreeing with whatever troublesome stories my mom was saying about me.

Mom didn't understand me. She didn't know how lonely I felt in a house filled with people.

She didn't understand that the only reason I ran out of the room today was to protect my new best friend.

My dog, Paisley.

Paisley

Lessons I learned today on my second day of third grade.

1. No matter what anyone tells you, do not chew markers. It will not end well for you or the markers. I now have purple lips and purple fur surrounding my mouth.

2. Listening to stories is my new favorite thing to do. Harper and Paz read me books from the library today and I could've listened to them all day. My favorite was about a pigeon wanting to drive a bus. I've met a few pigeons and let me just tell you, none of them wanted to drive busses. Mostly, they just wanted to eat bread off the sidewalk and poop on windshields.

3. We did a science experiment on the different states of matter than involved a piece of candy and some soda. I was so terrified when I saw what happened that I hid in the closet until I knew the experiment was over.

4. Sometimes, the best way to show someone you care is to make sacrifices. Thank you, Stuart. I owe you a big slobbery kiss tomorrow.

Paz

I'm not exactly sure why I decided to give Paisley a hug on my way out the door today. She was curled up on a bean bag chair in the corner and I just bent down and put my arms around her neck. She licked me and I didn't even try to wipe off the slobber.

Miss Little must've seen this happen because she came up to me to ask me if I was okay. I shook my head yes, but I wasn't sure that was true. Being in a family, with my awesome teacher and sweet dog, reminded me of all I was missing.

Was Uncle G really all the family I deserved?

Miss Little helped me get my things together and we lined up for the bus. She told Paisley that she needed to stay in the soundproof room until she got back from dropping us off. I wanted to so badly to take Paisley home with me. Uncle G and I would take such good care of her. I knew we would.

I started to cry small baby tears when I loaded the school bus. How can I love someone so much that I just met yesterday?

Unconditional love is a pretty powerful thing.

Miss Little

I really feel like I need to confess. I should just tell Mrs. McGee the truth. I should tell her that I snuck in a dog for the past two days and hopefully she will believe my sincere apology and not fire me.

I really want to do that.

But, I also know what is best for my students. In a few days, they have formed a bond with Paisley. She has become a new student and I can't tell my kids that she isn't allowed back.

I tried that once and Paisley escaped anyway.

I decide to quickly leave school as fast as I can. I pack Paisley into my giant duffle bag and hope that I don't run into anyone on my walk outside. The exit outside my classroom door provides the perfect escape. I shouldn't run into too many people on the sidewalk to the parking lot.

I'm almost in the clear. I pull out my keys to unlock my car when I hear,

"Miss Little, how is your day going?"

I look into my bag and quietly tell Paisley not to bark.

"Oh, hi Mr. Franklyn," I respond back to new teacher friend.

"Need a hand with those bags?" he asks.

I don't want to sound rude, but I also don't need to get caught with a canine. I kindly tell him that I am all set, but appreciate his willingness to help. I quickly open my car door and set Paisley's duffel bag in the car. I breathe a sigh of relief.

It's only Day Three with Paisley and I'm already exhausted.

Harper

Webster's Dictionary defines Cystic Fibrosis as, "*a very serious disease that usually appears in young children and that makes it hard to breathe and to digest food properly.*"

I've had cystic fibrosis all my life and it's still hard for me to understand. My mom says that it takes special kinds of people to live with CF, but I don't feel very special.

I just feel different.

After school, my mom takes me to the grocery store and on our drive over, I accidentally share a piece of information I swore to Miss Little I wouldn't say.

"I read to Paisley for almost twenty minutes today!" I say with as much excitement as I could muster.

"Who's Paisley?" she asks and I immediately regret even bringing Paisley up.

"Just a friend," I respond hoping that she won't ask anymore question.

But, I know my mom. She's a little bit nosy.

She then asks me how I met this friend and if this friend is a new student. I tell her that she is probably my new best friend.

I see my mom smile. Thanks Paisley, for not only making me smile, but for putting a beautiful smile on my mom as well.

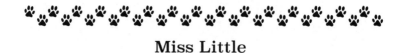

Miss Little

I take Paisley home, but immediately I feel guilty. I can't stop thinking about how much trouble I will get into if someone finds out that I have a secret classroom pet. It's not like a class fish or a class hamster.

This is a dog.

Paisley is a dog.

But, she's so much more than that. She's a helper. She's kind. My students can go to her when they are feeling down and she will comfort them. She will listen to them whether they are reading or reciting their math facts.

She's the kind of friend that everyone needs.

But why do I feel so guilty?

I fix dinner, correct papers, and struggle to keep my mind off of my dilemma. Do I continue to bring Paisley to school?

I toss and turn all night and by the time morning rolls around I'm exhausted. I fix myself a cup of coffee and scoop Paisley's food into her dish. I can tell she's excited just by the way she is looking at me and that's when I make up my mind.

Paisley has to come to school.

I probably should have left her at home.

Stuart

Well, that did not go well.

Mom took me home, but she hardly said a word in the car. I knew she was mad and to be honest, I was a little mad too!

I was used to being Stuart the trouble maker. In fact, one time, I think I overheard one of the teachers call me, "Stuart the Terrible," but I can't prove it. Miss Little didn't see me as that. She said I had a "brilliant mind" and that, "one day I could change the world."

That's why I needed to protect her. I needed her to be my third-grade teacher. She made me want to make good choices and work hard.

But I also knew that I needed to save Paisley, so I did what I did and I don't regret it.

I'm mad though, because Mom thinks I did an awful, menacing thing, but I was only trying to do the right thing.

When we pull into the driveway I ask Mom where Lily and Rose are. That's when she finally talks to me.

"They're at Grandmas," she tells me. "You and I need to talk alone."

Oh man. I really did it this time.

Mom pours me a cup of apple juice then she fixes herself a cup of tea. She sets my juice in front of me at the kitchen table. I must be nervous, I don't even remember walking in the house or taking my shoes off.

"Stuart," she starts and I immediately feel my face turn red. "You just can't keep this behavior up. It's unacceptable."

My mind flashes to the day Officer Morris showed up at my house. I thought that conversation was bad, but the look of disappointment on my mom's face right now, tells me that this is way worse.

Would you like to hear about why Officer Morris showed up at my house?

Well, it started when Max, Mark, and I were playing outside. We live on a dead-end street. The Bailey's live across the street. They are an odd couple that I think are losing their minds. Once, I saw Mr. Bailey walk outside with just his tighty whitey underwear on. Gross. I can't get that picture out of my mind, no matter how hard I try.

Mrs. Jenkinson lives right next door. She's what you might call "a crazy cat lady." I think she has fourteen cats, but I can't be sure.

Max, Mark, and I were supposed to be playing catch with my new baseball, but they decided that they would rather play video games.

Lame.

I was alone. Again. So, I decided to see if I could throw the ball all the way across the street into the Bailey's yard. The first time I tried it, I didn't make it very far. It didn't even leave our yard. (But my mom told me to never give up, so I tried again.) The second time, I threw that ball with all my might, and, much to my surprise, it smashed right into the Bailey's beautiful bay window.

They weren't home, so I figured that I wouldn't need to say anything.

"Phew, I thought. "They'll never know who did it."

But what I didn't know is that Mrs. Jenkinson saw the whole thing. She must've taken a break from petting her cats. The Bailey's ended up calling the cops after they came home to find their window broken and were afraid of an intruder. Officer Morris showed up and started questioning the neighbors and that's when they found out it was me.

I broke the window.

I disappointed my mom.
And today, I disappointed her once more.

She's tapping her fingers on the side of her mug and I look at her. She sighs and then takes a sip of tea.

"Stuart, this behavior just has to stop." she states in her firm Mom voice.

"But Mom, I was just helping Miss Little," I whine.

I can tell she's confused.

"How were you helping your teacher by running out of the classroom?" she asks.

Oh boy. I just messed up. Again.

I panicked.

Sweat starting to drip down my face.

"Oh, never mind," I say quickly, but I know my mom. She won't drop it.

"Stuart."

I run upstairs to my room. I need to come up with a plan. A plan that won't get my teacher into trouble and that won't get me sent to military school.

Harper

I didn't have homework tonight, so let me finish telling you my story about Rainbow Sparkles.

She decides that she needs to find a way to successfully defeat Drake the Dragon in order to save her beautiful mane. She starts to run away from Drake, but he then uses his spicy hot sauce fire breath to try to stop Rainbow Sparkles.

Luckily, Rainbow is able to pass a little gas to push the fire back toward Drake the Dragon.

Just when you think Rainbow Sparkles is in the clear, Drake picks himself up and chases her again. She stops to take a sip of the magic water from the Sparkly River. The magic water causes her to grow in Super Giant Rainbow Sparkles and now she has the power to shrink things.

So, Rainbow Sparkles shrinks Drake and teaches him that it's never nice to try to steal someone's beautiful mane or anything else for that matter.

The End

Jillie

I couldn't wait to go back to school. I just loved having Paisley. She was my first real friend since the move to Texas. Don't get me wrong, Harper and Paz were pretty cool, but no one seemed to know me like Paisley did.

Mom woke me up for school today. She told me she had the day off so she could drive me to school. I was immediately excited. I missed spending time with my mom.

After I got dressed, I ran downstairs where Mom had made me a special breakfast. She made me eggs, bacon, and toast. So yummy. And that's when Mom told me the best news of all.

She'd be picking me up early from school today, so we could spend some much-needed time together. After the move, I hardly ever saw my mom and I think that's why she felt this was important. She told me that school was important too, but sometimes a girl just needs to spend time with her mom.

Mom and I got in Mom's new car. I asked her how she liked her new job and that's when she replied, "Jillie-Pop, I love it."

I could tell she did. Her eyes lit up and a smile appeared on Mom's face almost instantly. I still had no idea what my mom did for work, but all I needed to know was that it made her happy.

When she dropped me off at school, she told me that she wanted to see my classroom when she came back later. At the time, I thought that was the second-best idea of the day, but little did I know, Mom's visit would ruin everything.

Hope

My tears started to fall the minute I got on the school bus. I didn't sleep well last night. I miss my old life. I miss my dad. I miss my mom being home, even if she was always yelling or crying. At least she was there.

I packed my own lunch this morning, since Mom wasn't up. A package of butter crackers, a juice box, and an apple were all that I could find. When the bus pulled up to my house, I wasn't all the way ready. I was still wearing my pajamas, but I got on the bus anyway, and that's when I started to cry.

This really stinks.

I could hear the kids on the bus snicker, especially the older ones. I found a spot next to a girl that smiled at me, but I soon found out that it wasn't a nice smile, it was a devious one. The whole ride into school she told me how ridiculous I looked and how I should've just stayed home. She tugged

on my pajamas and said that they were hideous. Then she claimed that her hands were burning because I must have a terrible disease for being so gross.

I continued to cry and nothing I did could make the tears stop.

Kids can really be so mean.

When I got to school, my teacher could tell how upset I was. She didn't ask anything, but simply put her arms around me and in that moment, I felt what I hadn't felt in months.

Loved.

Paisley

Miss Little and I rode all the way to school listening to a Brad Paisley song. She really loves Brad Paisley and I think that's why she gave me my name. When the new song comes on Miss Little wipes a tear from her eye and sings along with Brad:

> *"I can't change the world*
> *Baby, that's for sure*
> *But if you let me, girl*
> *I can change yours."*

She looks at me and strokes my head. She tells me that there will never be another day when I'll be alone. She's going to love me, unconditionally, forever. I lick her hand, just so that she knows the feeling is mutual. The song is true. Miss Little changed my world.

I'm going to love Miss Little forever.

Paz

Before I left for school today, Uncle G told me that he wanted to talk to me. I love to talk to Uncle G, so I was excited to hear what he had to say. I wasn't excited for very long.

"I want to tell you about your mom."

I've asked about my mom many times, but it's always been the same answer: "When you are older, I will tell you." Apparently, Uncle G thought I was older today.

"Right now?" I ask him.

"Yep," he quickly responds.

He sits next to me on the couch. He puts his arm around me and says,
"I wish I didn't have to tell you. I wish I could protect you forever, but I can't. You need to know what happened to her. "

A tear brushes down my face, but I wipe it away before Uncle G sees it.

"Your mom was ten years older than me and protected me like I was a lion cub and she was the fierce lioness. No one ever tried hurting me as a child, because your mom was always there to make sure I was safe.
Our father died before I was born and our mother worked three jobs to keep food on the table. Your mom raised me. She fixed me dinner every night, taught me my colors, and showed me how to ride a bike. She was a hero in my eyes. My best friend. She was pretty incredible, Paz, and you are so much like her.

When I was eighteen, I needed to get away from home. Your mom was living in a small apartment in Philadelphia, working part-time at a children's museum and part-time at a restaurant. She asked me if I wanted to go to college in Philadelphia and live with her. I didn't even hesitate. I started looking for colleges right away. It wasn't long until I got accepted to business school.

Two years later, she had you. She called you her "peace." Your mom didn't have an easy life in Philadelphia. She worked all the time, was tired all the time, and wasn't treated very kindly by your dad. In fact, most of the time, she was scared of him.

A few months after you were born, I graduated college early, and was offered a prestigious job in central New York, right where we live now. (Well, to be technical, about forty-five minutes from where we live right now.)

I didn't think twice about accepting it, but I could tell that your mom was saddened by the news. She was my best friend and I was hers.

I begged her to come with me, but she wouldn't.

I'm still not sure why."

Uncle G stopped right there and wiped tears from his eyes. He took a picture out of his wallet and handed it to me.

It was my mother and Uncle G standing in front of our house and my mother was holding a little baby. Me. I stared at the photo while Uncle G continued talking,

"One day, your mom had dropped you off with me for a weekend. She said that she wanted us to do manly things like build birdhouses and ride tricycles. (I told her those things weren't super manly, but she still asked me to do them). By then, your dad had left and she wanted you to have a father figure around.

She told me that she would pick you up around dinner time, but she never showed up. I called the police to explain my concerns and they told me about a really bad car accident. I later found out that your mom was the one that passed away in the car. She was driving too fast down a winding road. She lost control of her car and crashed into a tree.

I held you in my arms and cried like a baby. Your mom was a special lady and so are you kid."

I didn't say a word. I gave Uncle G a hug and went outside to catch the bus. Uncle G asked if I was okay, but I didn't answer.

How do I tell him I'm not?

Stuart

I had to write an apology letter to Mrs. McGee before I was welcome to come back to school. I told Mom last night that I realized what I did was wrong and will find a way to make it right. I delivered the letter by myself this morning and Mrs. McGee told me that she was ecstatic that I realized that I made a mistake and learned from it. She said that's what all great learners do and she told me that even grown-ups make mistakes.

I'm not sure I believe that though.

I walk to my classroom and everyone runs over to give me a hug, even the girls. I'm a little nervous when they do, because I don't have an updated cootie vaccine. I really need to get one soon.

Even Paisley runs over to tell me thank you. She kisses me right on the cheek and I start to giggle. I usually only giggle when I'm playing a hilarious prank on someone.

Our dog was really changing me.

Harper

I shared my Rainbow Sparkles story with everyone today during our first ever "Sharing Session" during our morning meeting. Miss Little told everyone that it's necessary for our classroom community to spend time getting to know each other.

Jillie loved my Rainbow Sparkles story. She told me that it was a nice reminder about sticking up for ourselves and that it doesn't pay to be mean.

I smiled a lot. I was pretty proud of my work.

Paisley came up to me and sat down next to me. She really is such a good dog. We are so lucky that Miss Little is crazy enough to bring her to work each day, well at least for the past three days.

I wonder how long it will take for anyone to notice that we actually have a classroom dog. We've had two close encounters with Mrs. McGee this week and that was quite scary. I sure hope that doesn't ever happen again.

Hope

After my teacher gave me a long hug, I went to my seat, opened my journal, and started writing. I wrote about how upset I was that my dad left. I wrote about how scared I felt when I was left alone. I wrote about how hurt I felt when the girl picked on me during the morning commute. I even wrote about how loved my teacher made me feel just by hugging me this morning.

She gave me hope. Hope that everything in my life was going to be okay.

That's when I knew that I needed to give hope to others.

So, I decided right then and there, I was going to be a teacher one day. Teaching was going to be my destiny.

Jillie's Mom, Annie

Jillie probably hasn't told you why I decided to move our family from a busy life in Texas to a small, quaint town in central New York. I've always been a city girl and for the most part, I loved it. I could tell Jillie loved it too, so that's why it was difficult to make the decision to uproot our family from the hustle and bustle of city life to a quiet life in the country.

But when your dream job, pretty much falls into your lap, you have to take it.

So, I did.

My dream job meant a lot of long hours and time spent away from my family. I hardly saw them during the week and on weekends it was always laundry and cleaning. I knew I needed to do something fun with Jillie today, so I planned on picking her up from school and taking her to see my office.

I wasn't planning on what happened though.
Not at all.

Miss Little

The students spent the morning completing STEM challenges and I had to remind Paisley that we don't eat the marshmallows. The children had to create a tall structure using spaghetti and mini marshmallows. By completing this STEM challenge, students would strengthen their collaboration skills as well as their math skills by measuring their structure after it was complete.

Being a teacher is awesome. My students are awesome. This life I live is awesome.

Oh, excuse me for a second, I have to remind Paisley to not eat that marshmallow.

"Paisley, please stop eating the marshmallows. If you need a snack, I'll give you a doggie biscuit."

Sorry about that. It has been a little noisy in here this morning, because the students are doing a great job communicating about their project. That's why I don't even hear the knock at the door or realize the fact that someone, rather two people, have just walked in.

Mrs. McGee

The mom of our new friend Jillie, came to pick her up early from school today. I decided that I would walk her to Jillie's class since she was new to our school.

On our walk, we talked about Jillie and how she was settling in quite nicely. I tried knocking on the door, but there was such a ruckus coming from inside that I doubted they heard me. I explained to Jillie's mom that often times students work together to enhance their learning and sometimes their learning gets loud.

I finally opened the door to lead us into Miss Little's class. I couldn't believe my eyes. Miss Little had a dog in her classroom and she had **not** asked my permission before doing so.

Oh this was not going to end well, for her.

Jillie's Mom, Annie

There's a dog in Jillie's classroom.

How on earth is she supposed to get any learning done,

if she is spending all day entertaining a dog?

This principal is not looking too happy right now.

I think I'm going to get Jillie and leave as soon as I can.

YIKES!!

Miss Little

I guess I should've known this was going to happen. I knew I couldn't keep a dog hidden in my classroom. The look Mrs. McGee gave me reminded me of the look my mom gave to me as a little girl. I knew I was in trouble. Big trouble.

Major trouble.

Mrs. McGee told me to take "the dog" and go home. My students started crying. Jillie gave me a sympathizing look as she hugged me tight. Stuart told me he was sorry and that he couldn't wait to see me tomorrow.

I didn't have the guts to tell him that I probably wasn't going to be allowed to come back tomorrow.

Or the next day.

Or the day after that.

How was I a teacher for four days and already messed up this badly?

Jillie

I cried all the way to the restaurant where Mom and I were having lunch. I couldn't stop crying when I ordered my chicken tenders and broccoli. I tried not to cry while sipping my lemonade, but I couldn't help it. My tears kept falling.

Miss Little had to leave school today and it's all my fault.

If my mom hadn't come to pick me up, Mrs. McGee would not have had to visit our room, and then she never would've found out about Paisley.

And Miss Little would still be teaching. That's where she belongs.

Mom, we should've stayed in Texas.

Paisley

I don't know why I had to leave school today. I was behaving myself. I didn't chew anything I wasn't supposed to or pee on the carpet. (Believe me, I did think about it once or twice.)

Miss Little was crying. Uncontrollably. Sobbing. I started to whine too, just so she wasn't the only one in the car crying.

That's when she says, "Aw, Paisley-girl. It will be okay."

I believed her words, but I don't think she did. She wouldn't be okay unless she was back in her classroom doing what she was born to do.

Teaching precious children.

Stuart

I couldn't believe what had happened. Mrs. McGee just kicked Miss Little out of her classroom. Can she even do that? I'm calling a lawyer. (Do you happen to know any lawyers?)

I made stinky faces to Mrs. McGee all afternoon. She was our substitute teacher and let me just say that I missed Miss Little even more. She was strict, a little too strict if you ask me. She wouldn't even let us use the special markers to practice our spelling words. Miss Little would've let us and then I probably would've actually done my spelling work.

Paz and Harper cried for a good twenty minutes after Mrs. McGee kicked our favorite teacher out of our classroom. I was too mad to cry. I spent my afternoon figuring out how I was going to get Miss Little to come back.

Mrs. McGee

After I put the third graders on the school bus, I went back to my office so I could call my boss, the superintendent, Mr. Bryant.

I explained the situation to him. This is pretty much how our conversation went

Me: Hello, Mr. Bryant. How are you?

Mr. Bryant: I'm great, Mrs. McGee. How are you?

Me: Well, Mr. Bryant. I have some discouraging news. One of our new teachers, Miss Little has been keeping a dog in her classroom this past week.

Mr. Bryant: Oh my. Are the children okay?

Me: Yes, the children are fine. They are devastated that I made their teacher and their new dog leave today.

Mr. Bryant: Understandable.

Me: I'm wondering what I should do, Mr. Bryant.

Mr. Bryant: I would need to talk to our Board of Education, but first I would like to have a talk with Miss Little. I'm thinking she probably had a reason for doing what she did and I don't think it would be fair to her if we didn't at least ask her for her side of the story.

Me: Sounds reasonable. Anything you'd like me to do?

Mr. Bryant: Call Miss Little and ask her to come back to school in an hour. Tell her to leave the dog at home. I'm highly allergic.

Me: Thank you Mr. Bryant. Goodbye.

Right after I hung up with Mr. Bryant, I tried calling Miss Little, but she didn't answer her phone.

I knew she was upset. I'd be upset too. In fact, I was upset too! She could've at least asked to have a dog. I thought I could trust her, but now I'm not so sure.

Mr. Bryant wanted to meet at 4:30 and at 4:15, Miss Little finally called me back. I explained to her the situation and she said she'd be here as soon as she could.

Good luck, Miss Little. You are going to need it.

Paz

Great. Another person that's important to me just left me. Actually, a person and a dog.

My dog. Our dog. Paisley.

I just learned how my mom died just this morning, so I was already upset when I arrived at school. Paisley was comforting me while I worked through our project. She made me laugh when she tried to eat the marshmallows. She even licked my face when she saw a tear fall from my eyes.

Dogs are pretty amazing creatures.

Uncle G knew something was wrong when I ran up to him as fast as I could the minute I stepped foot off of the bus. He hugged me as tight as he could and just let me cry. When I explained to him what happened, he made a phone call. I didn't know who he was calling, but I knew it was important.

That's when he said to me, "Don't worry kid. We will make sure your teacher still has her job."

Uncle G is a lawyer.

Harper

Today was far from being sunshine and rainbows. Mrs. McGee called my mom after school to explain what had happened during school today. I don't understand why Mrs. McGee was so upset. Paisley just wanted to learn too! She was a great dog and she was our friend.

Mrs. McGee wasn't very nice to our friend or to our teacher.

When Mom hung up the phone, she came to talk to me. She gave me a hug and asked me how I felt about the whole situation.

I told her that I thought it was the opposite of how I felt about rainbows and unicorns.

I even said a naughty word.

(Well, you may not think it was a naughty word, but my mom hates the word diarrhea and every time I say it, she says I owe her a quarter.)

Although, I will tell you we have gotten pretty creative when we actually do have diarrhea, but we can't say the word.

My favorite is when mom calls it the runny mess from your backend. She once called it that when I was having trouble breathing and I'm pretty sure I almost died.

Anyway, sorry about that. What were we talking about?

Oh yes, I remember. Mom and I talked about how important Buster was to our family and how she thought it was a wonderful idea to have a dog at our school. She told me that's exactly what she told Mrs. McGee.

She then kissed the top of her forehead and said,

"Don't worry baby girl, we will make sure Miss Little is here to stay."

Hope

Fast forward approximately fifteen years from the day my teacher made me feel so loved. I'm sitting on a soft chair in a college auditorium. They are about to read my name. I am about to graduate with a teaching degree. I am about to change the world.

I begin to tear up when I hear the speaker read my name, "Hope Emilie Little."

Miss Little

Mr. Bryant's office is very big. My heart starts thumping away and I'm trying so hard not to cry. I feel the tears coming on, but I push them back. This is not the time to cry.

"Good Afternoon," Mr. Bryant says. He tells me to have a seat at one of the chairs by his desk. I'm starting to feel the same way Stuart must've felt when he had to go to Mrs. McGee's office. Brave kid. He did that for me and for Paisley.

"Miss Little, would you mind telling me why you brought a dog on school property?" Mr. Bryant asks.

I tell him the truth. I explain that Paisley followed us in line one day during recess and that same day she jumped right into my car. I mention the fact that she whined so much that I had to take her to school. She was used to being abandoned and I didn't want to put her through that again.

He seems to sympathize when I tell him about the fact that Paisley ran away from home to school yesterday and I didn't have a choice but to keep her in the classroom.

He then asks, "What about today? Why was she in school today?

I felt a giant lump form in my throat and I knew I had to tell the truth even if I could not teach any longer. It was the right thing to do.

"I brought her," I say, "because the children love her and they learned so much from her."

"I see," he states, as he writes a few things down on a piece of paper.

He soon tells me to not come to school tomorrow. He says that he and Mrs. McGee have to sort some things out.

I walk out the door and sit in my car.

I don't drive though, I can't.

My tears are blinding.

What have I done?

Uncle G

I am a lawyer. You may have read that I went to business school, but a few years ago, I decided to go to law school. I wanted to make sure Paz knew he could be anything he set his mind to. I've made a lot of mistakes in my life, but I want Paz to know that it's okay to learn from your mistakes and grow from them.

I contact a few of my lawyer friends that are pretty hesitant to get involved in a "sticky situation" case like this one. Because some students are allergic to dogs, it could end up hurting Miss Little, instead of helping her. Plus, we also don't know if this dog was up to date on all her shots, which could also be very harmful for Miss Little's case.

Paz and I chat about the challenges that I'm facing. He tells me that he will take care of fighting for Miss Little and Paisley. He will form a plan with his friends tomorrow at school.

It's times like this, I wish his Mom was here, seeing what an amazing son she has.

I sure do love that kid.

Stuart

The next day at school, Miss Little is not there. I am so mad. I don't want to be here if Miss Little and Paisley can't be.

We have a new substitute. She has short, curly, and red hair and she asks us to call her Ms. Pam. I'm also pretty sure that Ms. Pam has red lipstick covering most of her teeth.

Today is going to be very interesting.

Ms. Pam is drinking her coffee at Miss Little's desk when Paz comes up to me with a note. I read it quickly.

"Meet me in our study buddy room in two minutes."

In case you are wondering, the study buddy room is one of the old music rooms that are completely soundproof.

I quickly and cautiously move to the soundproof room. I don't even wait two minutes. I'm a rebel like that. Paz is there with Harper and Jillie. He tells us that he's come up with a plan. Paz says if you believe in something strongly, you can make it happen.

We all believe in Miss Little and we believe we can help her.

Harper and Jillie start designing posters to save Miss Little's job. Paz and I start writing a document trying to convince Mrs. McGee to let Miss Little and Paisley return to school. I believe this is what teachers would call "persuasive writing." Miss Little just taught us that this week and it's a good thing she did.

Harper

Ms. Pam didn't even notice we were gone until lunch time. We literally spent two hours working on saving Miss Little and Paisley. Jillie and I created beautiful posters and Jillie told me how awful she felt about getting Miss Little in trouble.

During recess, the plan is to go to Mrs. McGee's office and present to her the information we had worked so hard on.

Wish us luck!

Stuart

I've gone to Mrs. McGee's office a lot. Last year, at least once a week. One time I went because I put super glue on the door knob and my second-grade teacher, Mrs. London, got stuck. I also went in first grade because I flooded the toilet on purpose just to see the little girls' reaction to pee water getting on their shoes.

I'm used to her office. I can tell you that she has fourteen stuffed teddy bears on her bookshelf. She loves collecting seashells and there is a picture on her desk of her with Santa Clause. I don't know why, there just is.

Harper is the first to walk into the office. Mrs. Grady, our school secretary, smiles and asks what she can do for us.

"We need to talk to Mrs. McGee," Jillie says proudly. "It's important."

Mrs. Grady can tell we mean business, so she called into Mrs. McGee's office.

"You have some special guests, Mrs. McGee," she states.

"Send them in," Mrs. McGee responds.

We walk swiftly into Mrs. McGee's office and immediately get to the point.

Paz is the first to speak.

"Mrs. McGee. We want Miss Little back and we are here to tell you why we need her and why she deserves to keep her job."

Harper and Jillie show her their beautiful poster. One of them even managed to draw a portrait of Miss Little and it was pretty accurate. I was impressed.

Paz and I read our essay together.

Paz started cleared his throat and started to read.

"Miss Little is an amazing teacher. We believe that Miss Little is the greatest teacher we have ever had. We think that she should come back to our school, immediately."

I read the next paragraph.

"Miss Little is kind. On the first day of school she gave us a present. When we opened it up, we found that she had hand painted a little plaque with our names and the phrase, 'You can change the world.' Love, Miss Little. She was also kind when she welcomed a stray dog that was all alone, cold, and hungry into her home and our classroom. She wanted to teach us how to care for others."

Paz continued.

"Miss Little is smart. She taught us how to work together as a team and, based on our presentation right *now, you can see how much we've learned. She gave us cool strategies to practice our math facts and provided us with many different books that we could read. She knew what she was doing when she brought our dog, Paisley, to school. She was helping us learn more. By teaching Paisley, our math facts and spelling words, we were able to remember the information better.*

Miss Little is awesome. We all love her. She makes us laugh. She hugs us when we were scared or hurt. She encourages us when we feel like giving up. She is my favorite teacher. "

I blurted out. "She's my favorite teacher too!"

Harper and Jillie agreed.

We finished our presentation and headed out the door. All we could do now was wait and cross our fingers that Mrs. McGee had changed her mind.

Mrs. McGee

I couldn't believe what I had just witnessed. I called Mr. Bryant right away and said we had to speak to our Board of Education. The Board of Education is made up of citizens in our community. They make decisions that impact our school. They also decide what should happen to a teacher that brings a dog into school.

I knew what I wanted to do. Mr. Bryant agreed and so did our board.

Miss Little was able to teach our students so much in a short time.

Four days to be exact.

Imagine what she could do in a year.

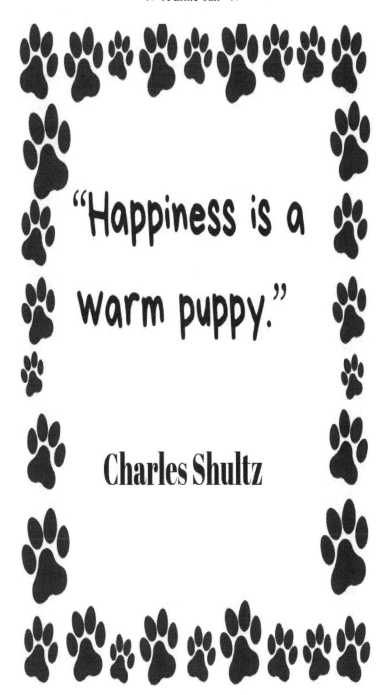

"Happiness is a warm puppy."

Charles Shultz

ABOUT THE AUTHOR

Liz Wise is a library media specialist in upstate New York. She loves reading, country music, laughing, and teaching.

She hopes to one day bring her dog Paisley to her school and (hopefully) not get fired.